SUSPICIOUS TIMES

ELVIS AND THE TIME TRAVELLERS

BY

MICHAEL LECKIE

TABLE OF CONTENTS

Acknowledgements

My inspiration comes from Australian author Greig Beck, who has written over fifty novels. I was introduced to the Alex Hunter Adventures by reading my first Greig Beck novel, Beneath the Dark Ice. Greig has published thirteen novels featuring Alex Hunter. Additionally, he has written other series, including the Primordia Series, the Centre of the Earth Series, the Matt Kearns Series, the Mysterious Island Series, and the Cate Granger Series.

Military to Author

Michael is a man who has dedicated 33 years of his life to serving his country as a member of the Australian Army. Throughout his military career, he advanced through the ranks, ultimately achieving the prestigious rank of "Warrant Officer Class Two" before being promoted to "Captain".

Michael's service took him to various postings within Australia, where he gained valuable experience and developed a deep understanding of the challenges and complexities of military life. However, the most significant and impactful period of his career was his service in Iraq during 2004 and 2005.

Despite the challenges and dangers of serving in a war zone, Michael remained committed to his mission and strived to make a positive difference. His dedication, courage, and selflessness are a true testament to his character and unwavering commitment to serving others.

Today, Michael is a proud veteran who continues to inspire others with his incredible story of his service. His experience and expertise make him a valuable asset to his community and a respected member of his profession.

After publishing his first novel, "Survival," in 2024, Michael has decided to unlock his previously unseen writings, introducing "Suspicious Times: Elvis and the Time Travellers."

The Journey Begins

COVID-19 ruined many lives when the pandemic closed the world in January 2020. Joshua and Samantha had never met due to the COVID-19 pandemic. They had planned to meet that year in June, but international travel quickly disrupted their plans, and we had to wait fourteen months to meet. They made the very most of the limited time they had. The date was May 26, 2021, and they would finally meet face-to-face.

Joshua just landed at Edinburgh Airport, walking up the aerobridge towards International Arrivals to pass through customs and collect his suitcase. Passing through customs, he looked around the airport. The hum of conversations in the airport, the occasional call over the intercom announcing arrivals and departures. The glow of airport signs reflected off polished floors, his suitcase rolling smoothly over them. Taking notice of the overhead signs, he headed towards the exit, but not before grabbing a coffee from Starbucks, the bitter yet comforting scent of fresh coffee filling his senses. Coffee wafted from his cup as he strode to the exit, feeling the air outside against his face. The air was fresh as he walked along the footpath towards the taxi rank. He walked up to a taxi with the words BRUCE on the roof of the car. Ensuring the suitcase fitted into the boot, he sat in the back as the driver asked, "Were too Pal?" in a broad Scottish accent. Josh listened intensely, then gave him the address. The driver quickly said, "You're from New Zealand". A little snicker from Josh said, "No mate, Australia". Driving out of the airport, a few roundabouts, then heading towards the motorway towards Stirling. The rhythmic clicking of the taxi's turn signal as it merged onto the highway took in the sights, and the conversation went on for a few more minutes. Then, the talk stopped. Roughly thirty minutes passed before the driver turned into the car park of the hotel. "Here we are", the driver said, "Twenty-five pounds, please". Josh handed over thirty quid, allowing the driver a five-pound tip. Josh got out of the taxi, grabbed his bag, and said his goodbyes to the driver, who smiled and drove off. The chill in the air was a bit fresh considering it was about seventeen degrees. Looking at the building in front of him, he took a deep breath and summoned the courage to walk into the front door. Josh, not needing to open his phone up to read the text message, politely said to the young girl at reception, "Just heading to room 118, I'm expected." Nodding her head, she opened the door with a switch under the counter. Walking up the stairs, Josh approached room 118. Taking a deep breath, all was about to change for Josh. He knocked on the door. She opened it slowly but quickly, if that makes sense. Their eyes met, and he took a deep breath and, as he had always done, said, *"Hello, beautiful,"* as he had always done when she sent a selfie or a picture with her in it. She grabbed his left arm, pulled him inside, and leapt into his arms as if in one motion. They kissed for what seemed an eternity. He thought to himself that from this moment on, the deal was done. He knew, as did she, that they had to be together; two and a half years of seeing each other via a phone was too much to handle - the real deal was the deal. We made love three times in the short time we had. Each time was better than the last, if that was ever, if that was even possible. Smelled. They talked for what seemed like hours. That day was truly beautiful in many ways. What began as a longing had finally become reality. Yet now, in November, we found ourselves not arguing with each other but struggling within, both of us had distanced ourselves from our partners to the point that our time together, however fleeting, would have to end. Joshua had to leave and return home, but not before we made plans to meet again.

Three months later.

Josh had moved into a self-contained two-bedroom apartment in Coffs Harbour. The apartment is just enough for what I need. A bed and a lounge room, not quite big enough to swing a cat in. He had been saving where he could as he planned for a holiday of a lifetime in Hawaii. Our savings would ensure we could survive while

Days turn into weeks, and weeks into long, long weeks. Text messages, along with video calls, would keep them in constant contact with each other daily, and they would often fall into a trance, pondering what they had just said and done. You open it, and it's.

"Hi Sam, been missing you since we said our byes. I have been, as you know, working on an idea, and I believe we can make this happen."

"Do tell," Sam replied.

Not one for long-winded messages. Nor

Josh typed back, "I have something planned and want to discuss it soon with you?"

"I'm intrigued," she typed back. Their conversation went back and forth for a few more texts, Samantha not thinking about the mystery.

Joshua's last message was, "When we talk next, I will get more details of the surprise for you. Love you, and talk soon, my love."

A few days later, Josh texted, and Sam replied. He knew she would be close to her phone, as the time was approaching 10 am.

"Hello, beautiful. Hi handsome. They talked and talked for an hour before they even discussed the surprise Josh had planned. "Sam, is your passport good to go?"

"I renewed it just before it expires in June, hun, why?"

Josh replied, "Let's video call." After a quick exchange of greetings, he asked, "Would you like to meet me in Hawaii?"

Shocked at first, it took Sam a few seconds to realise what he said. Before she could answer, he said, "I would love for you to join me in Hawaii. January 12, to be precise."

"I'd love to; this place is freezing that time of year. Plane ticket, how do"

I stopped your sentence.

"I'll email you the travel agent's address, the flight details, and I'll transfer the money into your account, and ensure you book the following flight with Virgin Atlantic as detailed in the email."

The email binged, and as she read it on her phone, she realised the flight was some 26 hours. Still shocked, they finished the call, and that afternoon, Sam went to the travel agent and booked the flight, which cost €1,129.75, with additional fees, of which Josh was aware. That, which cost €1,129.75, including extra fees, had transferred the money into her account. Now the waiting game: tickets booked, accommodation booked. Come on, tickets booked, accommodation booked. Come on, 12th of January, for the flights to begin. Your Sam's flight is leaving early that morning; mine, Josh's, and mine are also leaving early in the morning, with mine at 8 am, all on January 12th. If I did, my calculations are correct, and there are no delays at either end. We should be arriving within an hour of each other. Christmas and the New Year came and went; we celebrated both with our face-to-face and video calls. They then celebrated Elvis's birthday by watching the same movie, A Change of Habit, and then Viva Las Vegas. The morning of the 12th, they packed the night before, checked every detail of the travel documents, including passports, and ensured everything was in order. They were packed, their passports checked, and their e-tickets loaded on their phones, each detail confirmed one last time. Josh ordered an Uber, then double-checked his reservation for good measure. Sam would not be leaving for another eight hours. You ordered a taxi, and just as you are, you are. You ordered a cab, and just as you were about to. Sam had arranged for her. Your sister says she will drive you to the airport.

A few weeks earlier,

Sam asked her sister if she would drive her to the airport. The conversation soon turned inquisitive, with Sam saying, "How did you know I was leaving?"

"I'm not stupid, Samantha; I have heard your conversations with Josh for some time now. Nice. From what I could make out, he sounds lovely. Kids? Where are you going?" she asked. "I will tell you all about him in the car on the way, Sarah, and thank you for driving me to the airport."

As you loaded the car, she lifted her two suitcases, the car, and her carry-on bag. She stopped and paused for a minute. As you look around, you feel a little sadness, as this will be the first time you will ever leave Scotland on a holiday by yourself. You shake the thought out of your mind with the simple word *"Josh"*. A smile comes across your face, knowing that in just over 28 hours, you will be in his arms and Hawaii. The warmth of a tropical island has already forgotten you, as you are in Scotland. Sarah starts the car up, and as the seatbelts are slung across the chest and clicked in.

"Well, tell me all about him." She says to you. "Well, you texted each other months ago," and then you tell her that you have been seeing me for over two years only via the phone. You purposely neglect to tell her that we met back in May last year. She looks puzzled,

"So, you have not met him; how do you know so much about him to trust him?"

As you explained during the short trip to Glasgow airport, she could understand how you fell in love, and I think she is also looking for someone like me. She accepted what you were doing, and as she walked with you to the terminal, she gave you such an enormous hug, which you had not had from her in some years. You both cry as you can feel her love for you returning.

"I'll be back, Sarah, and we will talk about Josh and us, I love you, sis. Look after mum, please". "You know I will, safe travels, Samantha".

Amsterdam

The plane lands in Amsterdam, but you cannot connect to the Airport Wi-Fi, so you cannot see the video message. You are feeling piss off that the Wi-Fi will not work. You reboard for the next leg, but not before grabbing a small bottle of champagne. Once on board, you look at your phone and realise it is still in Aeroplane mode. You quickly take it out of Aeroplane mode and connect to the Wi-Fi. The strength is not that good; you click on WhatsApp, and in one minute, the video message appears. You take a sigh of relief. As the plane is about to take off, you have to wait a little longer before you can hear the video. The plane levels out, and practically everyone on board reaches for their mobile phone. She reached for her phone from the magazine holder. As you open WhatsApp and click on the video, and with your earplugs in, you see and hear me.

"Hello, beautiful. I hope the flight is going well. If all goes according to schedule, you should be in Amsterdam. Well, I hope so. I am heading to Coffs Harbour airport and shall see you in Hawaii. I am so looking forward to seeing you, my darling. We are going to have a great time. See you soon, Samantha. I love you so much." End of message.

Both flights are in the air, and there will be no way to communicate for the next 10 hours. There is nothing to do except sleep and wait for the plane to land. You think of the song Promised Land and ask the pilot to set us down.

"This is your captain speaking. We hope that you have had a pleasant flight. We will be touching down at Honolulu airport in the next hour. Cabin crew; please prepare the cabin for landing."

The excitement hits you with a bang, as you know; I will be waiting on the other side of customs. The plane touches down; you disembark, ensuring you have compiled your entry documentation. You have your ETSA, and all that awaits you is to collect your bags and wait in line.

You clear customs, and there I am. The biggest smiles are on our faces. You look exhausted; don't blame you. As you come closer to the exit, we can't take our eyes off each other, and then you are in my arms. Seeing how tired you are, I've already got a trolley ready for our bags. I place your bags onto the trolley, ensuring they will not fall. We head to the taxi rank, holding hands, and then I bring you into my arms and hold you tight as we walk. We wait in line for the next taxi and put our bags into the boot. I tell the driver to take us to the Pacific Monarch Hotel. The time is 6:45 pm.

We arrive at the hotel, check in, and head to our room. Drop the bags off, and after a long and loving kiss, we head down to the restaurant. We are both starving. Only to find out there is no restaurant in the building. Not to worry, the Esplanade has plenty of dining places. We stop at a burger place, and we nod at each other. We ordered a couple of burgers and soft drinks. Feeling tired, we head back to the room. Trying to keep ourselves awake for a while so we can adapt to the time zone and shake off the jet lag. We are too tired even to make love. However, we kiss, cuddle, and hold each other as we drift off to sleep.

Morning in Paradise

WOW, we slept like two floating logs in the sea. The sun has risen, and we are bathed in sunlight. Feeling refreshed yet still a little tired, we looked at each other and smiled as we kissed, the sun's heat beaming into the room. Rubbing your body, I can feel the urge to do more and more than we did. Kissing your neck and rubbing my hands down your back, feeling for your butt, and then slowly reaching behind, I can feel the warmth and moistness of Eden. You move your hands around me, and as I fondle you, you do the same to me. Knowing we had not showered for some 37 hours, there was no oral sex, just a lot of kissing, and then I pulled you on top of me, and we just made love. We knew the best was yet to come.

We roll off each other after a little bit of fun, catch-up sex, and love is yet to come. Both rest and jet lag are almost gone. We showered, and as we did, we took great pleasure in washing each other; I think we spent around 30 minutes doing so. Washing each other and then cuddling, letting the cool water run over us. To feel each other after such a very long time apart.

"Honey, how about tonight we have a spa?"

"Oh, hell yes hunni".

"I see if there are some spa suds. If not, we'll buy some. We might do a little bit of shopping today."

"That goes without saying, hunni, I'm in Hawaii,"

We both laughed. As we left the shower and bathroom, now towel-dry, I put the kettle on as we dressed. You turn the TV on and listening to American TV is a little weird as the accent is more prominent than back home in Australia. The kettle boiled, and soon the coffee was ready for me. As you had asked for a cup of tea, I gave you your wish. We discussed the flights, and I was particularly interested in yours, as you had to go through several legs when you mentioned Amsterdam, and it took you a while to get the Wi-Fi to work until you had returned to the plane. We are dressed for the warmth that Honolulu offered, as we heard the temperature is 82 degrees Fahrenheit. Perfect temperature. The time is just approaching 10 am, and I motioned to the door.

"Shall we go and get a bite to eat somewhere and do a bit of that shopping you want?"

As we head out to Diamond Head Market & Grill, which was featured in a brochure in the room for brunch, the walk along Kuhio Avenue with the beach to our right looks marvellous.

"Sam, are you glad you came?"

As we look at the beach. You gave me a frown, as if to say, 'Are you kidding me?' Then said'

"How do you say, My Fur Coat, this is just beautiful, and being with you, my love, makes it just perfect."

I pulled you a little closer, if that was possible, leaned down a bit, and gave you a loving kiss on the cheek when you turned your head towards me, and kissed me on the lips.

"Always kiss me on the lips, hunni, always"

After a few seconds with our lips embracing each other,

"Roger that, baby, roger that. We are talking about these"

When you looked at me,

"Yes, these lips"

You raised a finger to indicate your lips. A slight chuckle escaped both of us as we kept walking down the road. You paused and said,

"Do you want to walk on the beach side?"

I nodded, and we waited for a gap in the traffic before crossing the road. Then a police siren, "Woop Woop," sounded, and we both looked left and right when we saw the cop car on our right. I point to my chest to indicate that it was us. He nodded his head in affirmation. We stepped onto the sidewalk and waited for the cop to get out of his car. Knowing how cops work, we made no sudden movements. As he walked over to us, his partner was standing on the other side of the car, his hand resting on his service revolver. In his broad American/Hawaiian accent,

"Good morning, sir and ma`am."

We both responded with *"good morning, officer"* When I asked,

"Have we done something wrong?"

He exclaimed that we had crossed the road illegally, and we needed to cross down at the lights or the closest crossing. He asked us as he heard two different accents.

"Where are you from?"

"I am from Australia and Sam is from Scotland".

"Well, if you could in the future, please cross the road at the lights, and crossing, we shall all be fine."

And with that, he turned around and headed off, as you said,

"Thank you, officer. Have a nice day."

We looked at each other and raised our eyes as you then said, *"We are naughty already,"* and we both chuckled a bit. We kept walking, holding hands and getting closer to the beach, commenting on how beautiful the beach and water looked, with medium-sized waves crashing onto the shore every twenty seconds or so. There was a stall nearby. We stopped in front and saw what I was looking for, a flower. I paid the $1.20 and then placed the flower on top of her right ear. I took out my phone and took a photo.

"The flower suits you, Sam, have a look,"

As I turned the camera around to show you the picture, I took the photo.

"Aww, it is lovely, hunni."

Reaching up on tippy toes, you gave me a quick kiss. She looked around at other items, but nothing at this stage interested her, and they moved on. Soon, they came across the Diamond Head Market & Grill without hesitation, looking for the road crossing to cross. Pointing to her right, she said,

"There, over there."

They hastened to the crossing and walked inside, waiting to be seated, as required by COVID regulations. A young waiter soon asked us how many were in our party, and they indicated two; he ushered them to a table outside and read the sign that stated we still had to be seated at least 1.5 meters from other customers. Socialising has been reopened, but they are still playing it safely with social distancing. You hand me a menu, and we both read it. You ask me, 'What would I like?'

"Eggs Benedict with salmon, please." "Coffee as well, hun," you say.

"Yes, please."

You get up, approach the window, place the orders, and then return to the table.

"What are you having, Sam?"

"Scones and coffee, hun."

"I read they sell out pretty fast, so I'd better try them."

The young lady, our waitress, comes out with a pot of coffee and two cups, places the cups down, and pours the coffee in. "Thank you", you tell her. You took a sip and almost spat it out. Under your breath, you say,

"This is shit." I don't bother trying mine.

The food is then delivered, and the waitress says, *"You don't like the coffee?" with a southern drawl. "No, it's not the best,"* I exclaimed. She appeared a little shocked, muttered a few words under her breath, and walked away. We looked at each other and shook our heads, giving a little laugh. The food was ok, nothing worth writing home about.

"Hun, let's not come back here, hey."

"I think we can strike this off our must-come-back list."

Just then, the waitress came back with two espresso takeaway cups and said,

"Sorry, sir, our coffee is an acquired taste for most of us islanders, and here are two espresso milk coffees. I think you call this one a Latte, and I noted you dear had black coffee, and here is a black coffee. We hope this will be to your taste; thank you, as she turned and walked back to the kitchen.

"Well, that was unexpected." We took a sip, and wow,

"This is coffee, really nice; how is yours, Josh?" "Excellent. Perhaps we might come back here after all."

Well, we finished our coffees and food, of which I took a small piece of a scone from you.

As he paid the bill, he then asked for directions to the leading shops, and Alana gave me a map of the stores and said,

"Grab a cab and head that way, mate."

She laughed at trying to sound like an Aussie.

"We'll head that way in a cab, and here is a map of the stores."

"Great, thanks, hun; you get the cab."

I've seen it on TV shows; all you do is whistle and raise your hand. So, I gave it a try, but nothing happened. I tried it again, and a cab pulled up. We climbed in, and he asked, *"Where to, buddy?" "To the shops on the main drag, please,"* and I pointed in that direction. A short ride and $10, including a tip, were paid, and we hopped out, stood, and looked around to soak in the shop fronts and think about which way to go.

"You decide, babe", this way, as you pointed to a large store. We walked and entered the Ala Moana Centre, dress shops, shoe shops, lingerie, you think of it, and it was all here. As we wandered around, going in and out of shops, until that one item caught your interest. You asked me to go away. I think I know what you're going to buy, so without hesitation, I turn and head out the door, waiting in front of the store. Ten minutes later, you come out with a bag and don't show me the contents. I didn't need to know, as I am sure I will get to see it very soon, or at least in the next couple of days. We went from shop to shop with a purchase here and there. Then I came across a shop that sold bath products.

"I'll be back in a couple of minutes." I came out with.

"Ooo, nice", you said.

"Let's see how this goes tonight, my baby girl", as I gave a wink.

We walked around for a couple of hours, grabbing a bite to eat and sitting inside a bar for a little celebratory drink.

The evening was quickly approaching, and we just wanted to keep walking around and taking in the sights. So, we headed to the beach and then walked back to our hotel. The sun was setting, and we stopped to sit on the grass right in front of the sand. We held each other, our arms wrapped around each other, our heads leaning and touching as we listened to and watched the sea crash against the shore, with the sun slowly setting. It was truly magical being there with my girl, "you said to me,

Josh, thank you for being in my life and for inviting me here. I am so in love with you.

We looked at each other, smiled, and kissed as the sun lowered into the sea.

The sea swallowed the sun, and night was upon us. The street and shop lights illuminated the road and grasslands, as shadows stretched across the sand to meet the ocean. The crashing of the waves is loud and romantic, as we got to our feet.

"Do you want to walk or catch a ride?" I said to you.

"How far?"

"At a guess, two miles, give or take."

"Can we take a ride? My feet are a little weary."

"Ride it is, then."

We walk to the crossing and wait for the green light to walk. The lights changed, and the hearing-impaired sound also indicated it was safe to cross. We crossed the street and then went to the taxi rank, where we said hello to a few locals, but they just looked at us as if we didn't belong there. I hailed a cab, and soon we were at the hotel's front lobby. Still keen to see inside the bag you are carrying, I offered to take the bags.

"OH, no you don't!"

You said, pulling the bag away with a playful grin before pretending to hide it behind your back.

"Shower and freshen up before dinner, sweetheart?"

"Yes, please."

As we head to the elevator, I ask the receptionist if there's a good steakhouse nearby. He recommends Hy's Steakhouse, just across the road, and hands me their phone number to make a reservation. We take the elevator up to Room 318. The room has been serviced, and the fridge is restocked, including fresh milk.

"Sam, I'll call Hy's Steakhouse and book us a table," I say.

"Okay, I'll jump in the shower," she replies.

"I'll join you shortly, Miss Sam."

"Don't be too long, it's only a quick shower."

As you walked towards the bathroom, you turned around and grabbed the bag.

"I wasn't going to look, truly," as my fingers are crossed.

I pick up the phone, dial 0 to get a line out, and then dial 808-922-5555. I have a reservation for 8:30 pm, which gives us fifty minutes. Since Hy's is right across from the hotel, we have some time. Without wasting any time, I go to the bathroom but see that you are already finished.

"That was a quick shower?"

"Told ya, hun, be quick"

As I dropped my strides and lifted my shirt, you gave me a quick kiss on my nipple.

Then said, "That's it for now," and walked out of the bathroom.

"Oi, you can't leave like that?"

Laughter was all I could hear. I showered, and as I yelled out to Sam that the reservation was for 8:30, Josh dried off and walked out into the bedroom; she was already dressed.

"WOW, you look stunning, sweetheart, absolutely stunning".

You blushed a bit and said,

"Thank you, hun, but I haven't put my face on."

"You don't need it, honey."

As you brushed me aside with a kiss and then went into the bathroom to do your face, I dressed, put on some Aramis cologne, and brushed my hair. I saw the bag and looked at the bathroom door, which was all clear. I softly walked over to the bag, and just as I was about to take a peek, you yelled out, "Nothing is in the bag," and laughed. "The thought didn't even cross my mind," I said, giving a slight cringe at being caught without you even looking out the door. Both dressed and looking quite the couple, we shared a kiss, and the taste of your strawberry lip gloss was charming indeed.

We walked across the street, stood at the door to Hy's Steak House waiting to be seated, when a waiter greeted us and asked,

"Do you have a reservation, sir?"

"Yes, Campbell."

"This way, please", as he checked his list.

"Hy's has an elegant, tranquil ambience; this restaurant is Honolulu's fine dining," the waiter said.

"Just look at this place, Sam. I think we are in the right place for tonight."

"This is Brill, hun; thank you again; I love it."

"Samantha, you are just perfect. Everything you wear suits you, and now, here, WOW. You are amazing, lovely, and just so adorable."

You stand up and we meet across the table, kiss each other, and then sit down.

"Thank you, Josh, you ain't so bad yourself, hun."

"Let's look at the menu, babe."

We ordered appetisers, including Seared Scallops with a pistachio–herb crust and Prosciutto Di Parma with melon, followed by Filet Mignon and Bone-in Ribeye with both Au Poivre sauce and seasoned vegetables. Dessert, we will wait on. The meal is served with a glass of Champagne and a Domestic Merlot. The meals and drinks come, and they cannot be faulted. We toast to each other and our new beginning. We spend about two hours drinking to our future, to our past, and to us.

We are both a little drunk now, and luckily, we only have to get across the road. *Spa time,* you whisper to me, and with that, we are up, paying the bill—$ 410. Oh well, this day has been in the making for some 710 days, and we deserve it. As we staggered and stumbled across the road and into the hotel, we laughed like school kids, at what, who knows. Just the mood we are in.

We got to our room, and as soon as the door closed, we were hugging and kissing like we had never kissed before. You start undoing my shirt, and I'm trying to undo your blouse when you pull back, waving a finger at me to say no, no, no. You go to the bathroom, and the color is blue, like the

Hawaiian waters. This magnificent satin teddy, in a minute, you come out wearing the new Hawaiian Ocean Teddy with garter straps. The color is blue, like the Hawaiian waters. This gorgeous satin teddy features a color scheme reminiscent of the Hawaiian waters. This magnificent satin teddy, featuring garter straps, is paired with black stockings that fall just above the knee. My jaw drops to the ground and hangs there for what feels like hours. I take a gulp and shake my head in disbelief at how sexy you look.

"Sam, WOW. You look magnificent, wonderful, beautiful, and so god damn sexy. Come over here."

I watch you walk towards me as you sway your hips from side to side.

"Hey stud, feel your way," quoting a line from her favourite movie.

I leaned above your head and flicked the bedside light switch off. The switch had to be flicked on and off several times for it to turn the lights off.

They tried to drift off to sleep, tossing and turning, not able to get comfortable,

"Oh shit, I'm too restless."

"Would you like a hot or cold drink, hun?" Josh asks.

"Beer, please."

"Beer it is, and I'll have one with ya", Sam replied.

As you roll off the bed, I slap your butt, and you tumble back toward me, landing in my arms as our lips meet.

"I love it when you slap my butt", with a smile on your face.

"Well, if you get up again and I can reach it, I'll slap it again for another kiss."

As you get up, you deliberately stay within reach and shake your tush as if you're on the catwalk. Then, falling back onto the bed, I give you a light slap.

"Anything for a kiss", you tell me.

"Hey, Sam," finally leaves the bed and heads to the bar fridge.

"What "Pop Quiz,

A. Does Sam love Josh?

B. Does Josh love Sam, or

C. All of the above"

"Hmm, let me see, hard choices this, hmm, hmm. C"

"Yes, you are correct."

You crack the top of the 500ml Kona Longboard Ale and hand one to me.

"Cheers, my love," you say to me.

"Cheers, sweetheart."

"Do you feel like that spa now?"

You look at the desk clock; it's just a tick past midnight.

"How about tomorrow, just after breakfast?"

"Sounds great to me," as we polished off the beer.

"Bed, the beer did the trick, hun. Hunni."

The lights are flicked off after one touch.

"This time, it worked," he laughed to himself. He slides back into bed, the covers are pulled up, and we bring our bodies close to each other and cuddle each other tightly and kiss each other, and you say, "I love you, see you in the morning, sweet dreams, and only of me."

"I have no one I would want to dream about, my love. You are good for me as I am good for you. I love you. Sleep well, honey," we said as we drifted off to sleep.

The Time Shift

Something strange happened in the room; they both woke up startled. As Josh reached for the light switch on the bedside table, the room seemed to be spinning, yet we did not feel like it was twirling. The light switch would not respond, regardless of how many times he pushed it back and forth. The room got faster and faster, yet we still seemed unmoved. Strange lights are coming from within the walls. Looking at each other, and before either of us could say a word, everything stopped. We sat there, dazed yet not dazed, when you said,

"What the fuck just happened? Where did that light come from?"

"I have no idea, hunni."

I got out of bed as you grabbed my arm.

"Let go, it's ok."

Sam walked to the window and motioned for Josh to look out. We both looked out and saw that we were not on the fifth floor; we were on the ground floor, looking into the side of a house. *What the fuck?* you said. Both are puzzled, searching for answers within our minds.

"Try the lights, hun," Sam asked.

Nothing. The lights did not work. We could see from the window that a grey sky filled with dark clouds seemed to disappear before our eyes, and the sun was shining bright, as if it were midday.

"Get dressed, babe; we need to get out of here and see if anyone can explain what is going on."

As we tried to shower, the water did not run. *Nothing is working*, so we just put on random clothes and then picked up our mobiles.

"No signal"

"What the fuck is going on?" You started to panic.

"Calm down, Sam; let's go and find someone who might explain or have some idea?"

As you opened the door, we stepped out onto the grass under our feet. *"What?"* Before I could say anything else, we saw a sign that confused us even further.

Honolulu 1973

RCA Records Tour Presents Elvis in Concert – Honolulu International Center, Sunday, 12:30 am, Jan. 14, 1973

We both looked confused, gazing at the sign. Then you took out your phone and took a photo.

"This is some weird shit, hunni."

Taking in the surroundings, everything seems out of place compared to what we had gone to sleep in.

Walking across the grassy area, we are now in front of the Honolulu International Centre, looking very confused. Looking around, it was as if Hollywood had come to town and set up the stage as a very elaborate joke.

Honey, are we dreaming, or have we been pranked in a way I can't believe would happen, or are we in 1973?

You look at me with eyes wide open whilst taking in what we are seeing,

"I think we are, but how?"

"All I remember is we fell asleep, and the room started spinning with lights coming from the walls."

"Where is the room?"

"Over."

As I pointed out, where we just came from, there was nothing but lawn.

"Let's go, and I don't know, ask someone."

As we walked down the main road, leaving the centre, the city of Honolulu was not as modern as we are accustomed to.

"This place is in the 70s, there is a café; let's go there, surely there will be someone to give us some answers."

We walk into the café, and everything is from the 1970s. For whatever reason, we are in 1973, as I pick up the newspaper and show you the date. Jan 13, 1973.

"Do you know what this means, hunni? We can see Elvis. We need tickets."

You start jumping with excitement at the prospect of seeing Elvis live; I must admit, I am super excited. People are looking at us strangely because of the clothes we are wearing, but they don't seem to care, as that was the attitude of the period. People accepted strangeness as the norm.

After a few hours of wandering the streets of Honolulu, we find the Box Office and ask if we can purchase three tickets. Fortunately, there are a few left. I pay cash as the American money has not changed that much—twenty-five dollars to see the King.

"Why three tickets, hun?"

"Two are going to be used, then the third is our souvenir."

"Smart thinking," you tell me.

As we walk around the streets, admiring the look and feel of the 70s, we want to buy things but realize we have very little cash, and our cards won't work here, so we have to be careful as we wander, taking in the sights and atmosphere. We head to the small group of shops, and with our combined $155.00, we need to be prepared; we could be stuck here for a while. I suggest we head back to the International Centre soon, as we should find the room since this may be our way back to 2021. As we browse the shops and buy a few souvenirs—who knows what could be valuable when we return home?—we head off up the road when we hear Elvis playing, and it's coming from the International Centre.

"Shall we try to get in and take a look?"

"Why not, hun? Never say never. How good will this be if we can?"

Security personnel are stationed at the doors and patrolling the external areas of the building.

"Best approach is the direct one, Sam, let's see how we go."

As we approach the main door, Joe Esposito is coming out of the side door.

"Honey, Joe Esposito over there", as you point to him.

We head towards Joe, and as we approach, you say in an excited voice, "Hello Joe," and as soon as he hears your Scottish accent, his head turns. He heads our way, and as we come together, he says,

"Your accent Irish?"

With that, you quickly tell him.

"Nor Scottish man" in an aggressive but pleasant voice.

He apologises and quickly tries to appease us, introducing himself. We shake hands, and he says to me,

"I don't know that accent. Where are you from, Josh?"

"Australia, Joe," I tell him.

"So, you guys here for the show?"

We said, "We just dropped by and were lucky enough to get a couple of tickets."

After a little more conversation, he asked if we would like to meet Elvis. I think you almost fainted at that offer, your knees buckled a bit, and as I held you, we accepted without any hesitation. Joe reached into his pocket and handed us two passes. *"Access Back Stage"* is printed on them, accompanied by a small picture of Elvis and the dates.

Nervous as hell, we walked and talked as we entered the arena, and as the light from outside disappeared, darkness took over until our eyes adjusted. We could see the T-shaped stage, the large Elvis backdrop being displayed, and running through the programming.

"Exactly as it is shown on the DVD, hunni"

Joe says, "What?"

"Nothing", you say, realising we can't talk about what we know of the show. There on the side of the stage, Elvis and a few of the band members.

"Look, Sam, Elvis to your left."

As we neared the stage, the excitement was mounting.

Joe, do you have any water? I think Sam will need to take a drink; she seems a little excited, I believe.

"Sure, man over here. I love your accent, man, and yours, too, Samantha. Elvis is going to dig it too, and I can feel it."

He hands us a small glass bottle of water, and on the label, it says 'Elvis Live Honolulu International Centre, 14 Jan 73.' I whisper in your ear,

"Keep the bottle; this is one for our mantelpiece."

"Hell yes," you reply. Joe says,

"Let's go and meet Elvis," in his soft American accent.

Now the nerves are kicking in as we walk up the stage stairs.

"Elvis, I have a couple from, who are dying to meet you, Josh from Australia and Samantha from Scotland."

With that, Elvis turns around, and there in front of us is the King. *"Hello! Mr. Presley,"* I say to him, *"Elvis, please,"* he says back to us as we put out our hands to meet him. We then click a flash bulb, and another can only know seeing Elvis in person and speaking with him as the photographer takes several more photos.

"We are now in the history books," you say to me.

"Explain this one when we get back."

Elvis asks about our countries and mentions that he once stopped in Scotland on his way back from Germany. Then he adds that he would like to visit Australia, but the Colonel won't arrange it. As we keep talking, we ask him a few questions about the show tonight, which is a rehearsal. We ask if we can see his jumpsuit for the show, knowing full well what it is. Ronnie Tutt comes over, we introduce ourselves, and have a good chat with him as Elvis needs to leave. You say one last thing to Elvis,

"When you do the show tomorrow night, you might think about throwing off your belt and cape to the audience; any chance of throwing it our way?"

"Now that is a great idea, I might if I remember, where are your seats?"

I took out the tickets from my pocket and told him JJ 45 and 46.

"That's too far," I say as I look around the arena.

"He then says How about I give you my seats as I have also purchased tickets. They are just there," as he points to Row C, seats 1 and 2.

"Can that be the cape?"

"I will see if I remember, man."

"Elvis, wait!" you yell out to him.

"Can I have a hug and kiss from you, please?" you ask.

"Sure, Samantha, sure."

I could almost see her heart beating out of her chest. As you walked briskly to him, you both hugged, and he kissed you on the lips. The floodgates opened as tears ran down your cheeks; he wiped your eyes with his scarf and gave it to you. He turned and headed off stage.

You came back and joined Ronnie and me, then Joe came over. Joe said that the guys will be going into the green room, and if we would like to join them. We accepted without hesitation. We headed off, trailing Joe and walking next to Ronnie. He asked how we met, seeing that we are from two different parts of the world and a long distance apart. Trying to think on the spot, as we couldn't tell via the internet, which was not known, nor for civilian use, in this period.

"Well, Ronnie, we corresponded by letters, having once seen each other on a holiday I took to Scotland a few years back. We took a risk and met, and have been in love ever since. Our love for Elvis also brought us even closer."

"That's beautiful," he said.

We entered the green room, where we found J.D. Sumner and the Stamps, Jerry Scheff, James Burton, Glen D. Hardin, Charlie Hodge, John Wilkinson, Kathy Westmoreland, and the entire Joe Guercio Orchestra, comprising some 50-plus people. We just stood there and then entered Elvis and Colonel Tom. No one even turned a head except us. Elvis walked up to us and said, *"Man, have guys eaten yet?"* shocked that he would even talk to us, stammering to get the words out,

"No, no, just arrived and taking in all the members of your group."

"Well, take a seat, and we will have some food and drinks brought over to you."

We sat and watched as Elvis moved around the room, talking to anyone who wanted to listen, which they all did. We sat there holding hands, then occasionally pinching ourselves in disbelief. Elvis came back at the same time, and a waiter brought over a tray of sandwiches and some drinks. Alcohol was available if we so wanted.

"Elvis, tonight is a rehearsal. Would you mind if we stayed backstage and watched?" Then, without thinking, I said Love the songs you do!", realising what I had just said.

"How do you know what songs we are doing?"

"I saw a set list on stage", I came back with, knowing that to be a lie.

At the same time, you give me a little kick under the table and a *"what the"* look. Elvis then said,

"Samantha, I like the idea of throwing the belt and cape into the audience, and yes, I will throw the cape in your direction; good luck."

"It would be braw if I got it."

"Braw, what?"

"Good other words," you both laughed.

A person who later found out is Marty Pasetta, the director of the show, who yelled out, "Attention, Attention. On stage in five minutes!" With that, everyone got up and moved out. Elvis said, "Last rehearsal before the audience comes in. Joe, get those tickets for tonight."

With that, he got up, shook our hands, and kissed you on the cheek. There we are all alone in the green room with a plate full of sandwiches. We sat and filled our bellies. We quickly got up as the music started. We could see everything from the side, then moved to the seats, so we had front row seats to the dress rehearsal. They didn't play every song; instead, they played snippets to capture the movement of certain songs. Thirty minutes was all it took, if that. Everyone moved off stage to prepare. We ask Joe if we could see the American Eagle Jumpsuit. Joe said he would, and we walked to a second room, which had all the band and orchestra clothing for the show. Joe exclaimed that these costumes are all for the real show tomorrow night. We walked over and looked at most of the clothes, then at the jumpsuit. WOW, so pristine, it gleamed.

"Two suits used one for tonight and this one. Look at this, can we touch it?" I asked. "Make sure your hands are clean, please."

We both checked our hands and felt the suit. I was eager to take out my phone and snap a few photos, but I knew I couldn't. You cleverly distracted Joe, giving me a moment to quickly pull out the phone and take some shots. I snapped about ten photos, including one of you and Joe with the phone near my thigh. I shared that with you, and I hope you'll look at it.

After spending a few more minutes with Joe, we left the room, and with one last snap, I took a final picture. Then we headed to the side of the stage, where I quickly took some photos again, as many people were scurrying around doing last-minute tasks. The main doors to the arena were about to open, so we quickly moved out of the way of the camera crew and stage personnel. I could get better photos from here; I took shots of the crowd coming in and of the stage.

"These are better, honey."

You looked at me and gave me the biggest hug and kiss that lasted several minutes.

"Can't believe we are here and how, but I don't care, it is just so wonderful; we have met Elvis, Joe, Ronnie, and it is just the best. I am so glad we have met and this has happened to us. So fricken unbelievable. We can't tell anyone that is going to be so hard."

"Sam, when we return, I bet we will see ourselves in an Elvis book or magazine somewhere; remember the photographer."

"Shit yeah, perhaps the future has seen us, o' my god."

"I wonder if you or we get to catch the cape tomorrow night."

The lights dim; the band and orchestra take their places. After ten more minutes, the lights grow a little brighter. The drums start first, followed by the rhythm guitar, then the bass. The iconic opening theme begins. Goosebumps rise, the hair on my neck stands up, and then he walks out. What a figure he cuts. You're almost melting with excitement. Luckily, they are not playing 'Lawdy Miss Clawdy,' I whisper to you as you shush me. We stood there for the next hour, watching, listening, and applauding with every song and move he made. As the last song, 'Can't Help Falling in Love,' plays, we hug and hold each other, swaying with the tune. We kiss and hug in awe of simply being here, back in time. The show ends; Elvis walks off, as he usually does, with his customary salute to the crowd—raising his thumb and pinky.

Joe came and collected us; we went back to the green room, and this time there were about two hundred people there, including Jack Lord from Hawaii Five-O. We mingled as if we were important. Well, truth be known, we are time travellers. I took out my phone and snapped photos. You got close to Elvis, and he hugged you, and I took a very deliberate photo; this one is very special. Then the night went on for hours. Elvis left about twenty minutes after arriving, but we stayed talking to anyone and everyone we could, soaking up this once-in-a-lifetime experience. It was time to go as the green room started to empty. We moved outside with everyone else, and the relatively early morning air was a little fresh, as I said to you.

"A bit nippily for you, honey. You know what that means? I have to see firm nipples, rule one." As we smirked.

"Let us head over there; this is where we came from; maybe there is a door we just walk into?"

We moved across the grass, and we saw nothing that looked like a building or a door—nothing at all. We took one more step, and suddenly we were inside the hotel room. No lights, just the room exactly as we left it.

Both are feeling tired but not quite. I took out my phone to look at the pictures, and there they are. We thumb through them as we lie on the bed together.

"I'm too scared to go to sleep just in case we end up back in 2021."

We rolled into each other, and as we hugged and kissed, we just enjoyed what we had just witnessed. You started rubbing your hands over me, and I did the same to you. We had to make love in this time zone to add to the experience. Soon, we both had our clothes off and slid under the sheets; I don't know why, but the sheets soon came off as well. Our warm bodies take the chill out of the air. I'm not sure of the time, but when we woke up, we were back on the fifth floor in 2021. We looked at each other, and our faces showed the sadness of missing the Aloha Show. We sat there for an hour gazing out the window until the phone rang. It was the front desk asking if we were checking out.

I said to them, "Could we please stay one more night?" They agreed.

"Sam, perhaps we might go back tonight, who knows?"

We faced each other and lay there, gazing at each other. We both wanted to say something, but nothing was the best reflection of what we had just experienced. Then we smiled at each other, and then you told me,

"We need to shower."

"We do, honey, we do."

Without hesitation, we both got off the bed and, taking our clothes off as we walked towards the room, headed to the bathroom.

"Honey, I'll run the spa. I think a nice relaxing spa will do the world good."

"Josh, bring my phone. We need to see if we are in any pictures from there?" The spa was filling up, towels wrapped around our waists, and we sat on the chairs just outside the bathroom waiting for the spa to fill. Searching the net for pictures of the concert. I used my phone as well.

"Fuck," you yell out, "there we are."

And as sure as shit, there is the photo of us with Elvis on stage. We looked at each other with a frozen stare, and we looked again. No mistake, it was us.

"I wonder if anyone has ever noticed this. We will not know, honey, as our past is completely different from what it is now."

"Great photo, hunni. We have to get this printed and framed for our Elvis room. Who will ever believe us? How can we tell anyone that we time-traveled and had an input into his show?"

"Open YouTube and see if Aloha is there. We need to watch it."

"The Spa," I yelled.

Water was almost overflowing the spa tub. I quickly got up, handed you my phone as I moved into the bathroom, and turned off the taps. I reached in, pulled the plug, and drained some water. I added some spa oils and then told you the spa was ready. You brought both phones with you, handed me mine, and placed yours on the sink bench. We stepped into the spa, the water warm but comfortable. The water rose over the spa jets as we lowered ourselves into the warm water. The spa is spacious enough for six people, with a lounge area. You moved to the lounge part, and I sat next to you. You rested your head on my shoulder and chest as I pressed play on the phone. We watched the entire show—from the helicopter landing and the rehearsal shows—and then paused. During the band's introduction, just behind the Stamps to their right, you could see us, and there I was with my phone held waist high.

"How many people have looked at this footage?"

I scroll down to the comments section, and people are calling it a fake as they see someone holding what looks like a mobile phone. Some say it's just a notebook; others claim it's a portal to time travel, and some love the show. So, all in all, no one cares. I press play again, and we watch the finish of the rehearsal show.

The spa is lovely as the jets massage parts of our bodies. Your hand rests on my right thigh, moving in time with the music and occasionally squeezing. My right arm is over your left shoulder, gently caressing your breast without being annoying; our touch is non-sexual, just loving. The rehearsal shows end, and we are stunned to learn that we are now part of the Elvis DVD collection. Still don't know who in our circle of friends has any knowledge.

"We will not know anything until we leave this hotel, Sam."

"I'm getting out, hunni; I'm feeling a wee bit tired."

I look at my phone, and it is twenty past two; we both yawn. I stand up and lend a hand to assist you up and slap you on the left butt cheek as I stroked your thigh. You step out of the spa, I get up, and soon we are standing, towelling each other. Throwing the towels onto the towel rails to dry, I walk behind you, holding you by the hips, to the bed, kissing your neck. As we reach the bed, you turn around, plant a very loving kiss, and then fall backward onto the bed.

"Stud, take me now or lose me to sleep", you giggle.

We kiss with passion, pull the bed sheet up, hold each other, and say goodnight.

The sun is now peering through a slight opening in the blind. Josh feels the heat on his face. His eyes open, looking at the clock; it's around 10:15 when we wake up, and there's a collective sigh of disappointment because we're still in 2021 on the fifth floor. We get dressed after giving each other a morning kiss and cuddling. Throw on some clothes and walk to the hotel lobby, where you'll see other people moving about, then head to the breakfast bar. We take our time eating breakfast and having two coffees. You put your phone on the table, and with that, people start looking at us. Trying not to look like we are someone special, we stand up and head out the door, and people are still staring at us.

"What the Fuck are they looking at?" I give you a look of fuck knows.

I pay the bill, and then we head quickly out the door, and as we do, there on the counter, next to the door, is today's news, the Hawaiian Star Advertiser. On the front page is our photo. I grab the paper and read it in disbelief.

FAKE OR GENUINE TIME TRAVELLERS

There is a picture of us with Elvis, and another of me holding a mobile phone. There are press vans parked out front and a herd of reporters.

"To the lift, Sam," I scream softly.

We move quickly to the elevator, and as the doors open, a news crew steps inside. His head was down, and he didn't recognize us right away as he and his camera guy exited the lift. The doors closed when he realized who we were; he tried to open them, but it was too late. We reach our room and quickly close and lock the door with the chain. We go to the window, open the sliding doors, and step onto the balcony. Looking down, people are pointing and looking up. We step back,

"Fuck we know nothing of what they know about us. Have we become famous for time travel or as fakes?"

"Fuck knows, honey, fuck knows. Turn on the TV and see if anything is being said that will help us?"

Click on the remote and the tellie has come to life. We watch, and surely, within ten minutes, there is a crossover to one of the TV crews out front. We listen intently, and the reporter begins, "Behind me, up on the fifth floor, are Josh Campbell and Samantha McGregor," as he explains to the viewers that this photo bears a striking resemblance to these two individuals who are holding it up here. We only saw them for a Nano-second this morning, but they are here, and he would try to get an interview with either or both of us, as the camera pans up to our balcony, showing us standing there. It was a cross with a delayed feed. We held up in the room for the rest of the day, ignoring the numerous calls and banging on the door.

"Should we get the chance to rewrite the changes we have done, but how?"

"We need to try to recreate what we did the other night, I guess." You tell me.

"I can't remember what we did; we just fell asleep."

"Let's try that. Were the curtains open or closed, and were the lights on? The lights!!! Lie down."

We both lay down and I pressed the light switch on the bedrest, but nothing happened. I pressed it several times, but nothing happened.

"Shit, I don't know what else to do."

"Just let's go to sleep".

We closed our eyes, and within minutes, the room started spinning, with lights emanating from the walls. The room is plunged into darkness, and the lights stop spinning.

"We are somewhere, where thou?"

We get up from the bed, walk to the door, and there is grass; we have come back to the Honolulu International Centre.

"Are we back, and what date is it?"

"Let's go to the shop and look"

As we walk out, the "Elvis in Concert" sign is there, dated January 14, 1973.

"Well, we are here, but is it the 13th or 14th?"

You give me a sigh of relief that we have come back, and now we have to see when! We walk to the nearby café and look at the paper—January 13th.

"Ok, Sam, we have to NOT interact with Joe, and none of what happened back in 2021 will happen. Do you agree with me, Sam?"

You ponder over the question.

Well, we did meet Elvis yesterday. Check your phone to make sure we still have the pictures, please.

I take out my phone, flick open the Gallery, and yes, the pictures are there, but they may not be if we don't meet Joe, as it will not happen. You cup your hands and put your face into them. You say through your cupped hands.

"I might not recall this day, or will it just be that we will not have our photos?"

"I know, honey, we simply meet Joe, and do everything. I will not take out my camera on stage. We will not stand there on stage, make ourselves invisible, and stay for the show tomorrow night, then back into the room and leave, hoping we never appear in any photos. This will include the photo with Elvis, which cannot happen."

"Yes, let us do that, I want our photo with Elvis, we just have to ensure the photographer can't take that photo, or we have to destroy his camera."

The day went just like it did yesterday, which is today for us. We met Joe, and then on stage, the photographer took several pictures of us. I pay attention to where he goes. As he puts his camera down, I move closer and accidentally knock the camera to the ground. He cracks it, yelling his head off at me. I am fully apologetic, knowing we have just changed history again. The show continues, and we are deeper in the stairwell when Elvis comes off stage. He stops and asks what we thought of the show. Then, you said, "The show is magnificent and I think you need a haircut, Elvis." He turned to a nearby mirror and said, "Yes, I agree. I will." He shook our hands, gave a little kiss on the cheek again, and this time, a drop of sweat hit your lips. I saw your face light up with pure delight.

"Can I kiss you now?"

"No way, this sweatshirt is mine", with a smile.

Elvis had moved on by then, and we knew we might have reset the course of history; we hoped so. After the after-party, we decided not to go back to the room, as we wanted to see the 14th show. With only a credit card, we found a motel that was still open. We used the card, knowing it would work, as they had to use the old-style slider to record the card information, and it would be processed within several days. We would be gone by then. We started to fall asleep very quickly, as it had been an exceptionally long time, and getting up early was not an option, since the show wouldn't start until 12:30 am the next night. Joe had invited us back for 6 pm in the green room, and we could use the passes he gave us to re-enter.

"Oh, what a day, baby?" as we kissed and fell asleep.

Morning broke, and we slept in until there was a knock on the door. In a sleepy and raised voice, I said, *"Who's there?"* A soft, young voice replied, *"Room Service, Sir."*

"Ok, give me a couple of minutes, please."

"Ok, sir, I'll come back in twenty minutes. I'll do the next room. Thank you," she said.

I could hear the cart move away from the door. I leaned over to you and kissed your inviting, little, dry lips. You shook as if startled and quickly realised where you were. You licked your lips to add a little moisture and pursed them together, as if you were tasting a new shade of lipstick. Then you kissed me; this time, the kiss was more of a greeting than a startled one. *"Morning, handsome,"* you said as I greeted you with my daily *"good morning, gorgeous"*, and we kissed again.

"Room service is coming back in about fifteen minutes, so we need to get up. Would you like a 1973 coffee?"

"Black with a dash of cold, please."

"Coming up."

As the kettle slowly came to a boil, we both showered and dressed, and then there was a knock on the door. *"Room Service."* I opened the door, and there was this stunning young woman!

"Good morning, come on in."

"Thank you, sir", as she moves past me.

I try not to look at her curvy figure, as I know it's not the right thing to do. But I can't help it, I take a look, and then the look you give back could stop an elephant in its tracks. I smile and blow you a kiss. You roll your eyes.

"Breakfast, honey?"

"Yes, let's." You say in a deeper voice.

I give a little smile back. I move my head to the left to indicate that I want to move out of the room. We walk out and let her do what she does.

"Fancy the maid, hey?" you ask. She was somewhat cute but way too young for me.

Besides, I have the best woman a man could ask for. You shook your head and then kissed me as we entered the little dining room. We sat down and enjoyed some American bacon and eggs. The waitress poured us two cups of brewed black coffee. We discussed the show tonight, meeting up with Joe, and the possibility of seeing Elvis again before the show. I opened my gallery on the phone, and we looked at the pictures. Yes, they are still there, as they should be, including the photos and videos I took the day before we came back yesterday to prepare for the future.

"Well, if all goes to plan, we will hopefully have these photos and videos when we return home. Tonight is going to be fantastic."

"Hell, yeah, hunni, we are going to have the time of our lives, and we can't tell anyone."

"Well, we can, but not straight away. I'll have to write it in our memoirs."

"What's the time, hunni?"

"Just at midday, babe."

"So, we have a little time to sightsee?"

"Sure do, let's go."

With that, we stood up and paid the bill with the card on the merchant account's flatbed machine. Fortunately, no one has checked the expiry date on the card so far. We left the Jack in the Box takeaway and walked down Kapiolani Boulevard toward Kamakee Street, realizing it was a long walk to any shops. A taxi rank was nearby, so we caught a cab, which only cost $5.50, and we gladly paid it. The ride was only a few minutes long when we arrived at Ala Moana Boulevard and stopped at the parklands.

We spent the rest of the afternoon shopping for clothes for tonight and then stayed on the beach until 4 pm, soaking up the warmth of the day. We headed back to the place where the cab dropped us off and hailed another taxi. We traveled back to Honolulu, but the Best Accommodation probably isn't there in 2021, as this place is quite old even for its time. As we look out the window of the room, the Honolulu Arena is just across the street, and we know that a monument to Elvis will be unveiled on July 26, 2007.

"Just think, honey, we know exactly what is going to happen tonight. I wonder if we have interfered with history or not?"

"Time will tell, hun."

"That it will. Shall we shower as we are supposed to meet Joe at 6?"

"It's going to be a long day; how about we take a nap for an hour and then get dressed, 'cause I'm a bit tired from being in the sun too long."

"I'll set my alarm for 5.30."

The alarm was set, and we lay on the bed with the ceiling fan on the second speed, barely feeling the wind movement. The sound of the alarm rang.

"Wow, that felt like ten seconds, Sam; wake up."

It took several attempts to wake you.

"We've got about twenty minutes until we meet with Joe, shake a leg, honey."

We took a quick shower and got dressed in the clothes we bought.

"Hey, great choice of clothes, my dear; how's your Sam?"

You stepped out from behind the wardrobe door, wearing flare blue bell-bottom jeans and a pastel yellow embroidered tunic with a suede vest.

"Looks fab, you sexy cat."

I am wearing loon pants with a patterned shirt, with platform shoes and a huge belt.

"We need a photo, come on."

We take several shots in different poses and then realise my phone battery is very low.

"What's your battery life, honey?" "40%"

"Shit, we should have plugged them in."

"No time, I'll take my charger and see if I can plug your phone in the green room. You have to sit right next to it; we can't have anyone seeing it."

You take the charger out of our little travel bag and put it in my long pants pocket. It sticks out like a sore thumb,

"No good, need to carry it and find something to,"

Then you found a bag under the sink and handed it to me. We collected all our gear since we probably won't come back here after the show. We tossed out some items, making sure they could only be found if someone dug deep into the dumpster outside the arena. We approached the side door with our passes in hand; the security guard inspected the passes, then opened the door, and we stepped inside. We headed around the seats, passing the T section of the stage, stopping to admire it. The door to the green room was already open, and we stepped into almost silence. Everyone involved with the show was here, but they were very quiet.

"Must be pre-show nerves?" you say to me.

Joe is over there in the corner with several others. We move over just to let him know we are here; he looks up and gives us a warm greeting, asking if we could take a seat over there. He would join us soon and order whatever we liked. We did just that; it was gourmet food, and we only asked for water.

"This time we will try and keep the bottle hunni." You tell me.

"Well, I do have the bag. Can you see a power outlet?"

We are both looking around near Sweet Inspirations. Come over and tell us that we've had a seat change, and we're now in the seats Elvis said we could have. He will try to throw his cape to us. Then he tells us there's a full rehearsal in ten minutes, and if we want, we can watch from the seats.

I said, "That would be fantastic to see. We will. Thanks."

Joe excused himself because he had errands to run and needed to check on things before the show. The room started to clear out as everyone had to be on stage; this was my chance to plug in the phone. We moved tables and connected the charger. We couldn't leave the phone unattended, as it would cause a big problem if it was found. About fifteen minutes would be fine. We waited around twenty minutes, then heard the music start. We unplugged the phone, which now had 75%, enough for what we needed. We went out to the seating area and sat down. The rehearsal was fantastic; we knew we'd have enough power, so we recorded some parts of the practice. This footage has never been seen before. We know we can show it because it's easy to explain and can be found online. There are always videos from people's home cameras popping up. The rehearsal finished, Elvis left the stage, and the band stood up when the director said, "We need to record a few songs, so back on stage, people. Places." With everything done, everyone left the stage, and there were about ninety minutes until the doors opened. We stood around and moved about a bit, then I went back into the green room, grabbed a few more bottles of Elvis bottled water, and came back. Then, out of nowhere, Elvis appeared and came over to us.

We stood up, and the first thing you said was,

"You've had a haircut?"

"Yes, Samantha, thank you for the suggestion yesterday."

"It looks much better today, Elvis." You tell him.

We chatted about topics beyond the show, as he expressed genuine interest in Scotland and Australia. Elvis excused himself when the time came—the doors would be opening soon, and he was needed in the dressing room.

As the main doors swung open, the noise was nearly deafening. The crowd's chatter gradually settled into a hum of anticipation as people found their seats. The room carried the stale scent of smokers, an odor I've always found unbearable. Then the lights dimmed, and the opening notes of his theme music surged through the speakers. The audience buzzed with restless energy until a sudden hush fell over the room.

The opening strains of Also Sprach Zarathustra began, and we locked eyes, squeezing each other's hands. Moments later, Elvis strode onto the stage with that iconic swagger, acknowledging the roaring crowd before pausing at the microphone. For a heartbeat, he glanced to his left—almost as if he were looking directly at us. With his guitar slung over his shoulder (handed to him by Charlie), he launched into See See Rider, followed by Burning Love. We were giddy, bouncing in our seats like children, stealing kisses and embraces between songs.

Elvis was magnetic. The crowd—ourselves included—was spellbound. After Suspicious Minds, he paused to address the audience, introducing his bandmates. I leaned into you, whispering, "We're so lucky, darling. So frickin' lucky."

As A Big Hunk O' Love wrapped up, we braced for Can't Help Falling in Love. Singing along, we watched his cape sway with each step—closer, closer—until I positioned myself to catch it. Elvis unclipped the cape with practiced ease and flung it toward us. For a split second, victory seemed certain… until a towering Hawaiian woman barreled into me, snatching the cape midair. The fabric's edge whipped across my cheek, slicing deep. Blood welled instantly, streaking down my face.

But then—you dove for the fallen cape, clutching it before anyone else could react. We had it. A trophy and a battle scar. As bystanders lunged greedily, you shielded the cape like a lifeline. We bolted for the side of the stage, slipping behind the curtains into the green room. The cut demanded attention; I pressed a scrap of clothing to my cheek, stanching the blood.

"Sam, we have the cape; how is that for the best souvenir we could ever hope for?"

You are more concerned about my face as you add a bit of bottled water to the cloth and hold it tight against my cheek. After a few minutes, the bleeding stops. We hear the announcer say, *"Elvis has left the building. Thank you and goodnight."*

"I think we should do the same as you tell me."

"Back to 2021?"

"Yes, please."

We gather our bag and wrap the cape, using one of the tablecloths to disguise it. We then leave with the audience and, once outside, head left to our time machine room, where no one else can see us. We step into the vortex, which is our special room. We lay down on the bed and just talk about what had happened and look at the cape. We kiss and cuddle for a while, then, still awake, I press the light switch several times, and we are spinning with lights gleaming out from the walls. Within seconds, we are back to what we think is 2021. The room is now filled with lights from the ceiling and the sound of a busy street below. We get off the bed and open the curtain, and the fifth floor looks like the same place. I grab my phone, and the pictures are all there. I look at the time on my phone, and it changes from 02:10 to 14:16. What will the history books tell us?

We took a deep breath and smiled at each other.

"Sam, we have just witnessed the greatest performer of our lifetime, and to go back in time, how good has this trip been? You, coming here and being with me, and we found this switch that, when hit several times, took us back to 1973. How did this room or time vessel know?" he said.

"I can't explain it either; it is as if the room listened to us, and well, I am just glad we did."

She said excitedly as we sat up on the bed, we grabbed both our phones and opened the bag. In the bag was the cape, looking fresh as if it were just bought.

"No wonder they could never find it after the concert, and no one has ever come forth claiming it; we have had it without knowing it."

"I wonder how many times we have been here. The day before, we had the press outside, and we had to go back and correct a mistake. No press today, we have corrected it. Or have we," you exclaim.

Quickly grabbing our phones and checking the internet, we search for Elvis Aloha, but we don't see anything that looks different. We watch the online Aloha special and read the comments—nothing unusual. We read comments on the cape; still, no one has come forward. The phones need to be charged. We look at the photos taken. They're still there, showing us with Elvis on stage before the rehearsal on the 13th. You stood up; we had been almost motionless for three hours, watching and searching our phones for any sign of us back in 1973. There's a knock on the door, and you walk to it, opening it slightly. A middle-aged man dressed in a black suit, with a white shirt and black tie, stands outside.

He said, "Good afternoon, Mrs. Campbell. Would you and your husband, Josh, be so kind as to join us in the limousine?"

"Excuse me, who are you, and why did you call me Mrs Campbell?"

He gives a bizarre look,

"Ma'am, I, Clay, your driver for the last seven years, and the Elvis reunion is on today."

By this time, I have heard everything, and I have quickly looked up our names on the internet. A quick read showed that back in September 2020, it was discovered that we had travelled back in time and that we are now semi-famous. Today is the reunion, January 13th, 2022. We have travelled into the future by six months.

"Sam, please ask Clay to give us twenty minutes."

Clay leaves as you close the door,

"What is going on?" you ask.

"Sam, we have traveled six months into the future, and today is January 13, 2022. We're featured in all the papers for our time travel research, and we're famous. We got married four months ago, and according to the internet, we're now considered wealthy. I think if you open the wardrobe, you'll find clothes you never knew you had, and we're not in the same hotel. Look outside."

As you step to the window, we are some thirty floors up.

"Let us get ready and head down; we will find out soon; we just have to play up to everyone until we can make a little sense; we need to stay very close to each other, so we keep the same story."

"Sam, I can't put my finger on it, but Clay looks familiar."

"I haven't noticed, hun, in what way."

"I'm not sure, babe."

I took a sip of water from the ample supply in the fridge.

We quickly shower and dress; the clothes are quite expensive-looking. There is another knock on the door. This time, I answer it, and Clay is there.

"Sir, we must be leaving."

"Clay, we are ready, and I will just collect my things; see you in two minutes."

"I still can't think where and how I know him. There is something. Anyway, honey, are you ready?" I said as I picked up my phone and wallet.

"Wow, you look stunning."

"Why, thank you, Mr. Campbell."

We open the door and leave the room. Clay escorts us to the elevator, and we go to the car park. When the door opens, we see a long black limousine. Clay opens the back passenger door, and we climb inside. This car is huge, I say. Champagne in an ice bucket, along with four glasses. The other side door opens, and two strangers step in.

"Sir, the mayor and his wife, Mr. and Mrs. Caldwell."

After the pleasantries are exchanged, I offer them a glass of champagne as the car moves off.

As the Mayor speaks, we are discovering more about ourselves and what we are about to undertake. The car pulls up right in front of Honolulu International, and instant memories flood back from just eighteen hours ago. We step out of the limousine into a storm of photographers; luckily, the barricades hold them back. The flashes from cameras on phones and large cameras on poles illuminate the scene. Questions are shouted by multiple reporters; none are directed at the mayor. We wave and keep walking as Clay guides us past the paparazzi into the reception area of the International. On the way in, we notice large posters of you holding the Cape from 1973, along with numerous photos of us with Elvis, Joe, and other band members. You turn to me, point to the picture of the band with us, and tell me,

"I don't recall having a photo taken with the band."

"No, I don't either. This is going to be a strange night." As I leaned to whisper,

"Whatever happens, let's hope tonight turns out great," I say as I kiss you on the cheek.

Inside, hundreds of Elvis fans are gathered; the Aloha Elvis is playing on the screens. The mayor is speaking to us, but we can't hear him because we're too busy taking in what we're witnessing. You stop and ask him what he said. He repeats himself, and you tell me that we are seated over there as you point.

"That's where we caught the cape; do you think that's a coincidence, hunni?"

"I don't think so. A lot of effort has gone into this; look at the stage, and it's set as it was in 1973."

As we walk to the table, people stop and some start talking, but we can't hear what they're saying because the noise is deafening. When we reach our table, we notice that each seat has nameplates, menus, and decorations. I pull out your chair as you sit down, lean forward to kiss your shoulder, and tell you how lovely you look while you place your hand on top of mine and say, "Thank you, my Aussie Stud." I then take my seat to your left. We're facing the stage; the mayor and his wife are to your right, with Mrs. Caldwell sitting next to you.

We check the menu and the small table decorations, which are miniature Elvis statues similar to the bronze statue outside, erected in his honor. People begin taking their seats, and the noise starts to quiet down; it is now bearable. The man serving as the MC for the night walks on stage, the screens go blank for a moment, and his image replaces Elvis Aloha.

Mayor and Mrs. Caldwell, Mr. and Mrs. Campbell, distinguished guests, ladies and gentlemen, welcome to the inaugural Elvis Aloha Memorial dinner and show. First, let me say what an absolute honor it is to have Mrs. Samantha Campbell and Mr. Josh Campbell here tonight. I want to draw your attention to the screens around the room and present the Cape. The cape has not been seen since Elvis tossed it into the audience on January 14, 1973, until now. The story of how it came into Mrs. Campbell's possession is a tale that must be told. Tonight, we reveal that Mrs. Campbell came into possession of it, and you may find it hard to believe. Without further ado, I would like to play the exclusive interview we had with Mr. and Mrs. Campbell two days ago.

We look at each other with a confused look.

"This should be interesting, as you leaned over to me," whispering.

I pull my chair closer to you and put my arm around you as we look up at the screen. A large crackle came across the speakers, followed by the presenter's introduction.

"Welcome, Josh and Samantha," he starts.

"Thank you for having us." We spoke.

Can you tell us how you came across this lost cape from January 14th, 1973? The cape has been missing since then, yet you still have it. Given your age, it's hard to believe you were there, since you would have been 4 and 11 years old at the time. Was the cape handed down to you, or are you telling us you were present in 1973?

We both started to speak when you told me to go ahead.

"Well, Raymond, as you can see from the posters around the room and in the papers, you can see me and Samantha there with the cape and Elvis, Joe Esposito, and the band. Several universities and photographic institutes have authenticated these photos. The cape appears unstained except for the small amount of blood on the bottom corner and the scar you saw on my cheek." As I point to the scare. The bloodstain matches my DNA and has been dated back to January 14, 1973. We were there then."

"So, how did you get here then? Please do tell."

"This is the hard part to believe, yet it happened. The only part we will not reveal is where we, by accident, discovered a time loophole. We accidentally pressed a light switch several times; again, we will not reveal how many times or the timing. We are lying on the bed, ready for sleep, when the room starts to spin, and various coloured lights seem to be coming from the walls. When the spinning and lights stopped, there was no electricity, and no water from the taps. We opened the door, and we could see this building. At first, we saw the giant Elvis Aloha sign, and we had no idea where we were or what year it was. We thought it was impossible to travel back in time. When we viewed this building, it bore little resemblance to its current appearance. We went to a café not too far from here and grabbed the local paper, dated January 13, 1973. We met Joe Esposito, who liked our accents and gave us these backstage passes, which is the first time we have shown them. We grabbed a few more items from then, and again, no one has seen these until now. Here are two drink bottles, one still filled with the water from 1973."

You then mentioned how we first went there, and on our return, paparazzi were hounding us. We could only go back, change the past, and one of the changes was a photo of us getting a kiss from Elvis. That was in all the books when we realized. We have destroyed the film in the camera that took that photo. We have returned to the future. We are about six months ahead. We have no idea what happened here yesterday. We're probably the only people in the world who have time-traveled and have no clue how we did it. Waking up where we did and finding we're semi-famous is a shock. So, if we're at the function, it could be us, but not really us. Our bodies suddenly can…

With that, we disappeared, and then everyone looked at us sitting at the table as the spotlight shifted onto us. The mayor then stood up, and in response, the police moved in and arrested us so we could no longer time travel. Why had we set ourselves up? As we are escorted out of the room by two police officers, male and female, everyone stares and shakes their heads in disgust. We are being accused of false claims of time travel and the theft of historical items. We reach the police car and are placed in the back seat; our handcuffs are removed when the two officers remove their disguises and turn around. It was us.

We will explain once we're out on the road. Sit tight." You said to us.

We drove for about ten minutes, trying to ask questions, and all we got was silence.

The car pulled over on a side street. The lights were turned off, except for the interior light.

"We had to do that because we knew you guys—we would be exposed as fakes and frauds. Therefore, we had to go back and make a few changes. We only removed a few things from 1973, which you guys changed again when you went back. We still have the cape and those items we showed on the TV interview.

However, what had to change was coming back to this time zone. Now that we have ourselves, we can set the timeline back to normal.

By the way, you didn't recognise me—I was Clay. Sam, I thought you would have. It was Sam's idea to do most of this. She—you—worked it out that we needed to fix what you guys did by coming to this time zone.

So, what we're going to do now is go back to the room together. We'll go separately and meet in the room, lie on the bed together, and dream of what we have seen.

When we return to the concert, we must do one thing: attend the after-party, talk to Joe, and then, at 3 a.m., head to the room. There, we will become one, and everything will go back to normal."

We still have all the items, though we don't display them for anyone to see. Our lives are normal.

In 2052, all the facts come out, and we are dismissed as two fakes. The cape was never found, nor those bottles.

EPILOGUE

"Is there life after death?"

Samantha and Joshua lived a long and happy life until their passing, or have they?

Michael Leckie

THE END

www.ingramcontent.com/pod-product-compliance
Lightning Source LLC
Chambersburg PA
CBHW070454170726
48291CB00005B/1747